P9-ELF-678

ORNITHOMIMUS

AND OTHER SPEEDY "OSTRICH DINOSAURS"

Prehistoric World

ORNITHOMIMUS

AND OTHER SPEEDY "OSTRICH DINOSAURS"

VIRGINIA SCHOMP

New York

Contents

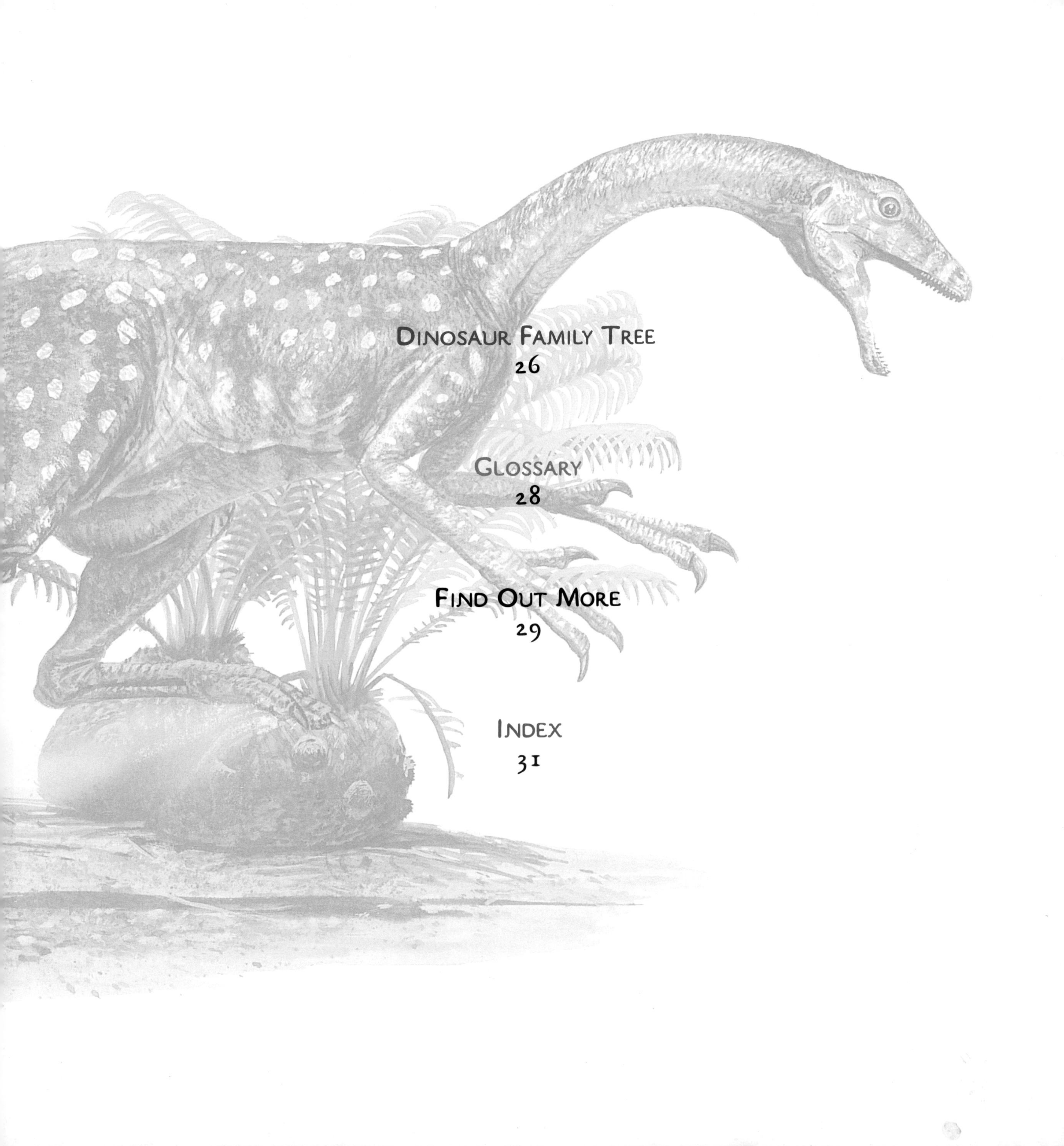

BUILT FOR SPEED

A group of hungry dinosaurs roams a vast green plain in North America, searching for food. They are *Ornithomimus,* some of the fastest animals on earth. These long-legged sprinters are not fussy eaters. One of the dinosaurs gobbles up berries. Another snaps at a juicy insect. A third pounces on a small lizard darting through the undergrowth.

Suddenly the hunters become the hunted. A pack of fierce tyrannosaurs attacks. The *Ornithomimus* run for their lives. Their long legs spring lightly over the ground as they try to escape the killers snapping at their tails. The giant meat-eaters fall farther and farther behind. Finally they give up the chase.

An Ornithomimus *shares a tasty fish with its hungry youngsters. These long-legged dinosaurs lived in the plains and forests of North America about 75 million years ago.*

This drawing shows an Ornithomimus *beside a modern ostrich. Both animals have rounded bodies, long legs, long necks, big eyes, and toothless beaks.*

Ornithomimus belonged to a small group of dinosaurs called ornithomimids. "Ornithomimid" means "bird mimic" or "bird imitator." These dinosaurs looked a lot like today's ostriches and other large flightless birds. In fact, *Ornithomimus* and its speedy cousins are sometimes called "ostrich dinosaurs."

The ostrich dinosaurs had long legs, necks, and tails. Most members of the group had toothless birdlike beaks. They also had big eyes and big brains. That probably helped them perform two very important tasks—hunting small animals *and* watching out for larger hunters with a hunger for ornithomimid meat.

DINOSAUR MATH

How do we know how fast *Ornithomimus* could run? To figure out the speed of living animals, scientists sometimes use a mathematical formula that compares the length of the animal's legs with the distance between its footprints. Paleontologists (scientists who study prehistoric life) borrowed that formula. They measured the fossils of ornithomimid legs. They studied footprints that they believed were left by an ostrich dinosaur millions of years ago. Their calculations showed that the dinosaur was running at least twenty-five miles an hour. That's about as fast as an Olympic gold medal sprinter, and it may be faster than any other dinosaur.

PICTURING *ORNITHOMIMUS*

If you wanted to draw an *Ornithomimus,* you might start with a gigantic ostrich. Forget the feathers. Give your dinosaur tough scaly skin instead. In place of wings, you'll need to draw two small arms and three-fingered hands tipped with long claws. To complete your drawing, add a long tail. More than half of this ostrich dinosaur's length was made up of its neck and tail.

You'll have to use your imagination to color in your drawing. No one knows what color dinosaurs were. Some were probably dull brown, green, or gray. Others may have had bright colors for attracting mates and scaring off enemies.

Ornithomimus *was the first ostrich dinosaur to be discovered. Long foot bones, long lower legs, and powerful muscles in the upper legs made it one of the fastest of all dinosaurs.*

ORNITHOMIMUS

(or-nith-oh-MY-mus)

When: Late Cretaceous, 75–65 million years ago

Where: Colorado, Montana, South Dakota, Utah, Wyoming, and Alberta, Canada

- About 13 feet long—as long as a small car
- Weighed about 360 pounds—as much as a very large ostrich

AVIMIMUS

(ah-vee-MY-mus)

When: Late Cretaceous, 85–75 million years ago

Where: China and Mongolia

- Slightly longer and heavier than a large turkey
- May have been covered with feathers

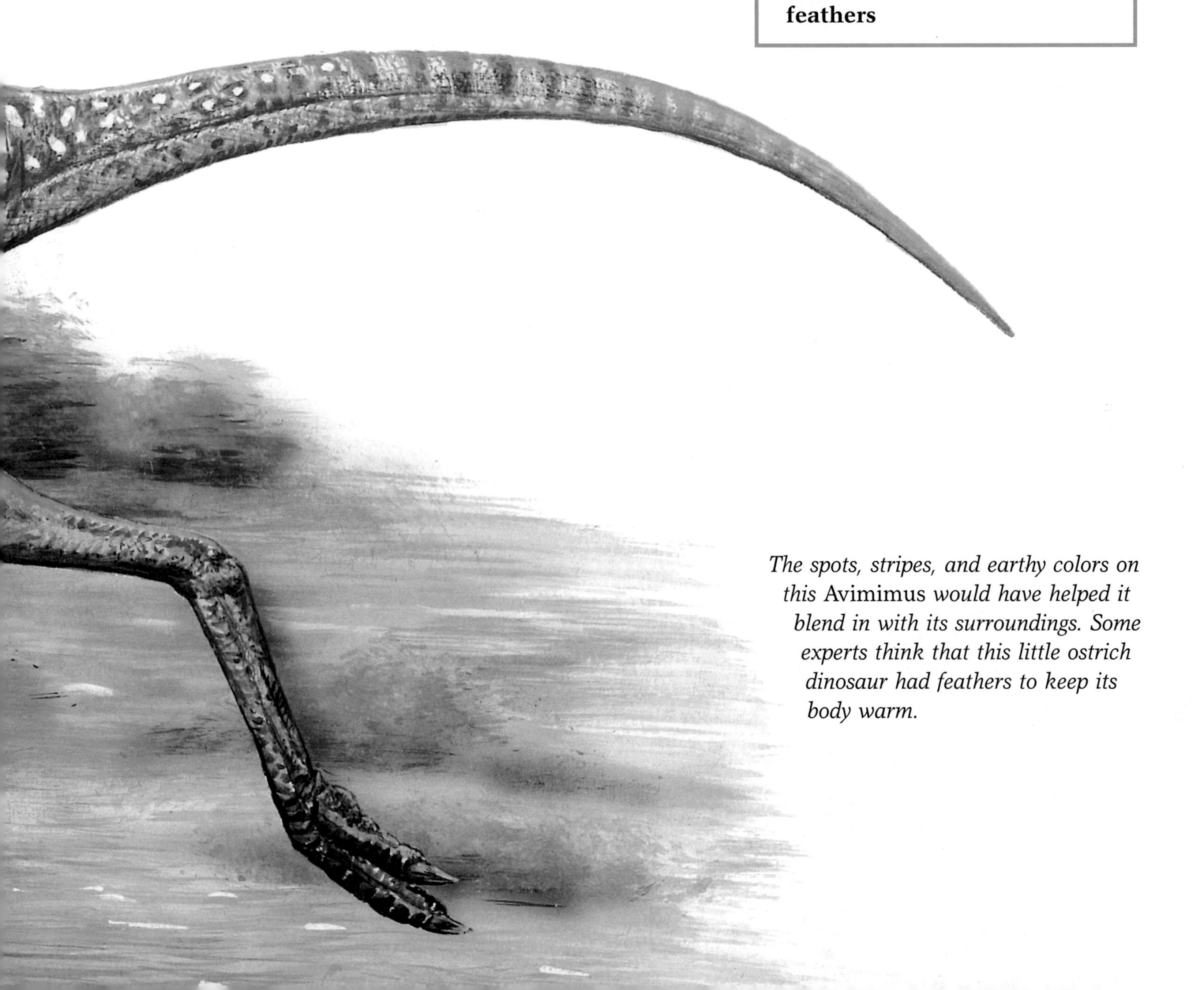

The spots, stripes, and earthy colors on this Avimimus *would have helped it blend in with its surroundings. Some experts think that this little ostrich dinosaur had feathers to keep its body warm.*

THE BIRD MIMICS' WORLD

The ostrich dinosaurs lived mainly in Asia and North America during the Cretaceous period. That stage of Earth's history lasted from about 135 million to 65 million years ago. During most of the Cretaceous period, eastern Asia and western North America were connected by a land bridge. Ornithomimids and other prehistoric creatures could walk back and forth between the two continents.

The Age of Dinosaurs

Dinosaurs walked the earth during the Mesozoic era, also known as the Age of Dinosaurs. The Mesozoic era lasted from about 250 million to 65 million years ago. It is divided into three periods: Triassic, Jurassic, and Cretaceous. (Note: *In the chart, MYA stands for "million years ago."*)

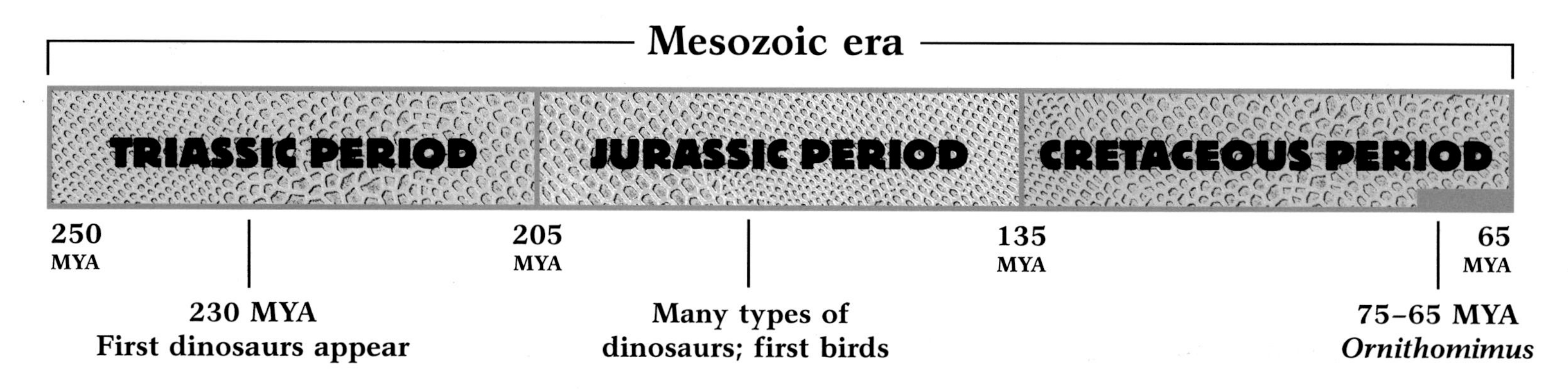

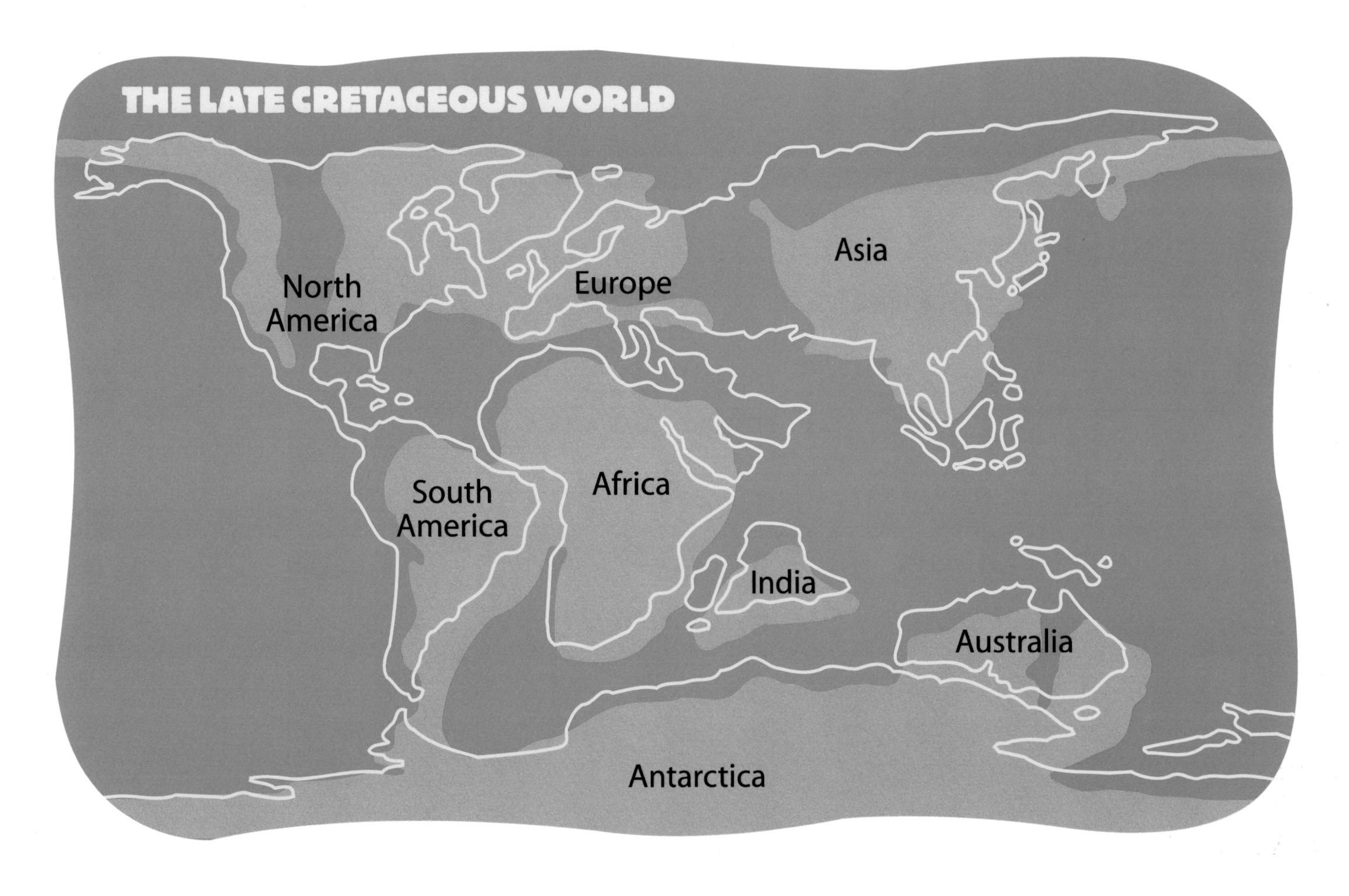

The yellow outlines on the map show the shape of the modern continents. The green shading shows their position about 75 million years ago, in the days of Ornithomimus. *If you look at the far right and far left of the map, you can see the land bridge that connected eastern Asia and western North America.*

Ornithomimus lived in western North America in Late Cretaceous times. If we could visit this dinosaur's ancient home, we would find a world very different from our own.

CRETACEOUS PLAINS

Our time machine travels back 75 million years, to what will one day be Alberta, Canada. The weather here is warm and wet. Trees, bushes, and ground plants cover a huge plain stretching mile after mile to the sea.

Dinosaurs flourish in this lush green paradise. We can see a variety of odd-looking creatures munching on the vegetation. There are swift two-legged plant-eaters. There are four-legged horned dinosaurs, duck-billed dinosaurs, and armored dinosaurs covered with bony spikes. Fastest of all are the ostrich dinosaurs, including *Ornithomimus* and its long-legged cousin *Struthiomimus*.

STRUTHIOMIMUS
(stroo-thee-oh-MY-mus)
When: Late Cretaceous, 80–68 million years ago
Where: Alberta, Canada
- Name means "ostrich mimic"
- Longer legs, arms, and claws than *Ornithomimus*

Extra-long back legs made Struthiomimus *one of the fastest ostrich dinosaurs. It looks like the leader in this footrace doesn't want to share its supper!*

As they feed, all these animals keep a sharp watch for danger. Wolf-sized predators with switchblade claws prowl the plains in fierce hunting packs. Even scarier are the giant tyrannosaurs. Three-ton *Albertosaurus* has huge jaws with long sharp teeth. In later years, this massive meat-eater's "grandson" *Tyrannosaurus* will become the world's most fearsome predator.

Albertosaurus *was a fierce tyrannosaur that first appeared in western North America about 80 million years ago. A few million years later, its descendant* Tyrannosaurus *was king of the dinosaur world. Little* Nanotyrannus *may have been a young* Tyrannosaurus *or a separate kind of small tyrannosaur.*

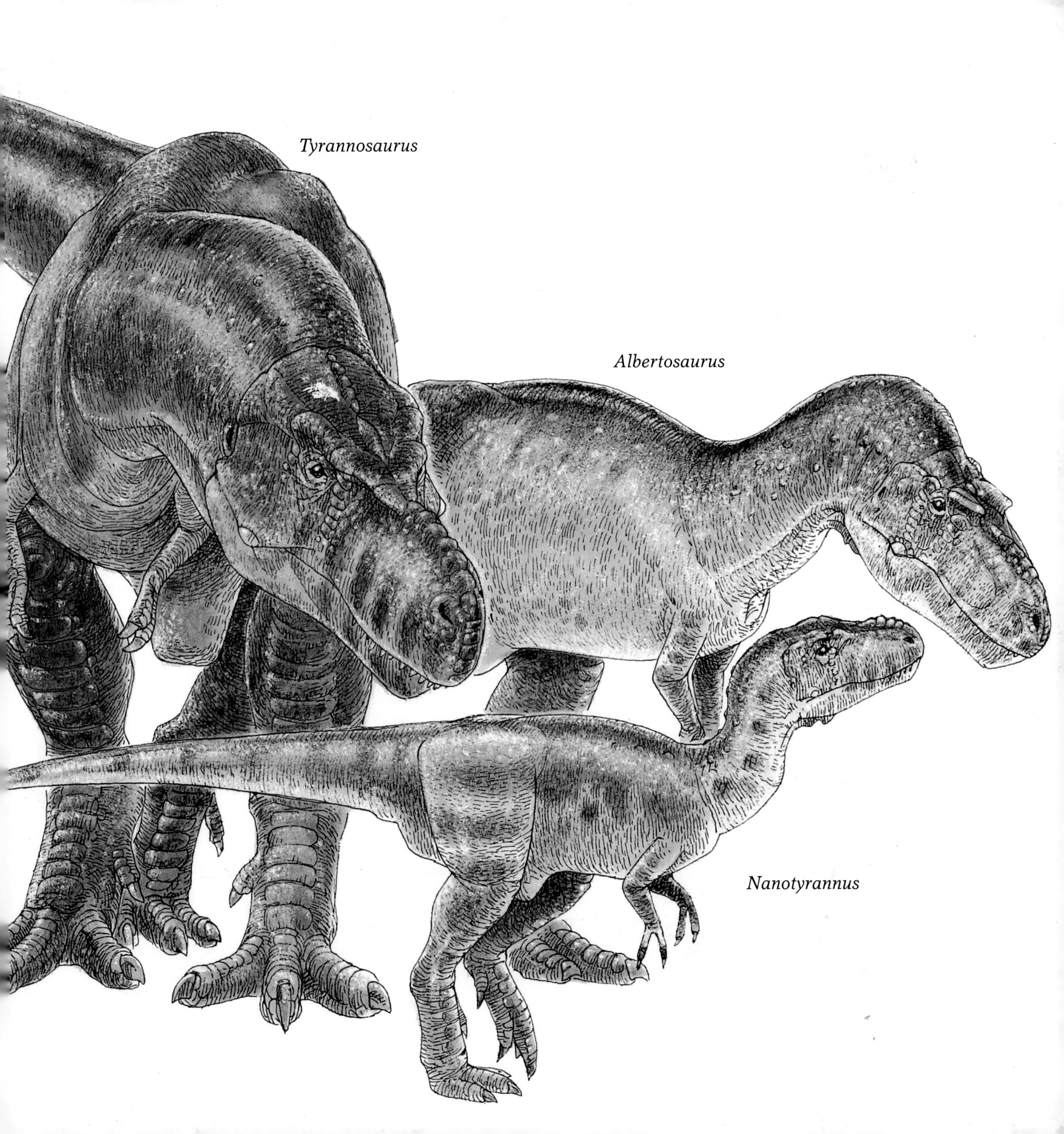
Tyrannosaurus
Albertosaurus
Nanotyrannus

ON THE MENU

Some paleontologists believe that *Ornithomimus* was a meat-eater. Its diet may have included insects, lizards, small mammals, eggs, and "left-overs" from animals killed by other predators. Other scientists say that the dinosaur was a plant-eater. They think that *Ornithomimus* used its long clawed fingers to pull branches toward its mouth. Then it snipped off the tastiest leaves, seeds, and fruit. Still other experts think that the ostrich dinosaurs were omnivores. That means that they fed on both plants and meat.

Ornithomimus *shared the North American plains with its cousin* Dromiceiomimus. *This dinosaur had exceptionally large eyes, which may have given it extra-sharp vision for hunting at night.*

DROMICEIOMIMUS

(droh-mee-see-oh-MY-mus)

When: Late Cretaceous, 75–70 million years ago

Where: Alberta, Canada

- Eyes bigger than tennis balls
- Longer arms and legs than most ostrich dinosaurs

No matter what it ate, *Ornithomimus* could not chew its food. That's because it had no teeth. Instead, it had a hard beak. Like many modern-day birds, the dinosaur could have used its beak to pick up and tear apart a variety of foods.

HARPYMIMUS
(har-pee-MY-mus)
When: Early Cretaceous, 125-100 million years ago
Where: Mongolia
- Primitive (less developed) ostrich dinosaur
- Flexible thumbs, possibly used for grabbing small prey

Harpymimus *was an early ostrich dinosaur with tiny teeth. Later ornithomimids replaced their teeth with a birdlike beak, which they used for gathering food, building nests, and many other tasks.*

SAFETY IN NUMBERS, SAFETY IN SPEED

Ornithomimus probably lived in small groups. The members of the pack helped one another find food and watch out for danger. Jogging across the open plains, they held their heads high. That gave their big eyes a far-reaching view of their surroundings.

When a hungry predator tried to put *Ornithomimus* on the menu, the dinosaur had only one defense. It ran! As its long legs pumped, its clawed toes gripped the ground like the spikes on running shoes. Holding its tail straight out behind helped the speedy dinosaur keep its balance as it raced to safety.

GALLIMIMUS
(gal-ih-MY-mus)
When: Late Cretaceous, 75–70 million years ago
Where: Mongolia

- **As long as an African elephant**
- **As heavy as 3 ostriches**

Gallimimus *was the largest known ostrich dinosaur. With its head thrust forward and its tail stretched out behind, it ran quickly over the Asian countryside.*

END OF AN AGE

Ornithomimus survived right up to the end of the Age of Dinosaurs. Then, about 65 million years ago, the last of the dinosaurs died out. No one knows what caused this mass extinction. Many experts believe that a giant asteroid smashed into the earth, filling the air with a blanket of dust. Over time, the cold and lack of sunlight may have killed the dinosaurs, along with many other kinds of animals.

Today paleontologists are constantly searching for evidence about life in the days of the dinosaurs. To learn about *Ornithomimus,* they study ancient fossils. They also observe modern-day birds, the dinosaurs' closest living relatives. Their discoveries add new chapters to the fascinating story of the fastest of all dinosaurs.

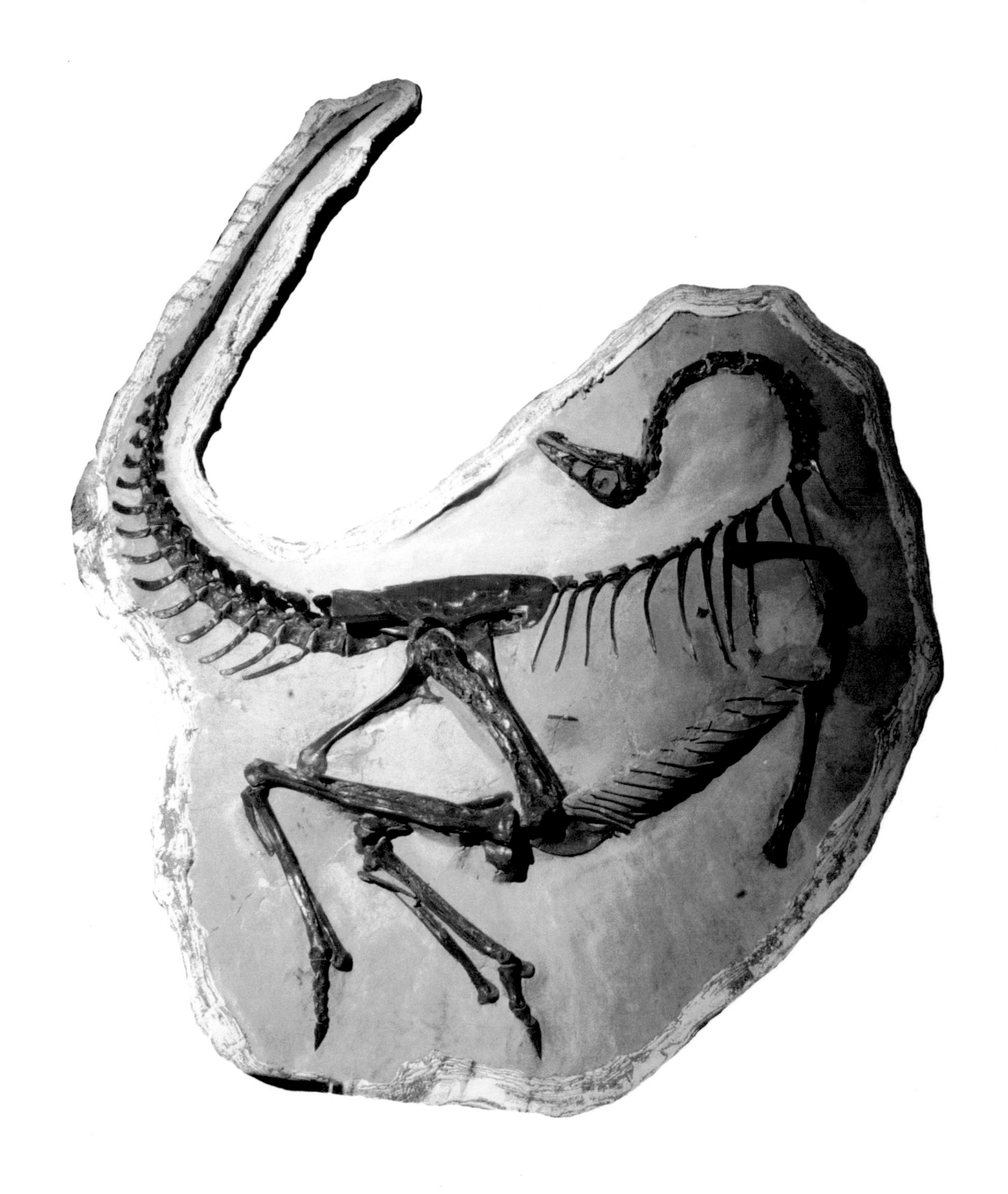

A team of paleontologists discovered this skeleton of Ornithomimus *in Canada in 1995. After the dinosaur died, its head and neck twisted backward as the soft tissues supporting the long neck dried out.*

Dinosaur Family Tree

ORDER

All dinosaurs are divided into two large groups, based on the shape and position of their hip bones. Saurischians had forward-pointing hip bones, like lizards.

SUBORDER

Theropods were two-legged meat-eating dinosaurs.

INFRAORDER

Tetanurans were theropods with stiffened (not flexible) tails.

FAMILY

A family includes one or more types of closely related dinosaurs. The ornithomimid family included fast "ostrichlike" dinosaurs.

GENUS

Every dinosaur has a two-word name. The first word tells us what genus, or type, of dinosaur it is. The genus plus the second word are its species—the group of very similar animals it belongs to. (For example, *Ornithomimus velox* is one species of *Ornithomimus*.)

Scientists organize all living things into groups, according to features shared. This chart shows one way of grouping the "ostrich dinosaurs" described in this book.

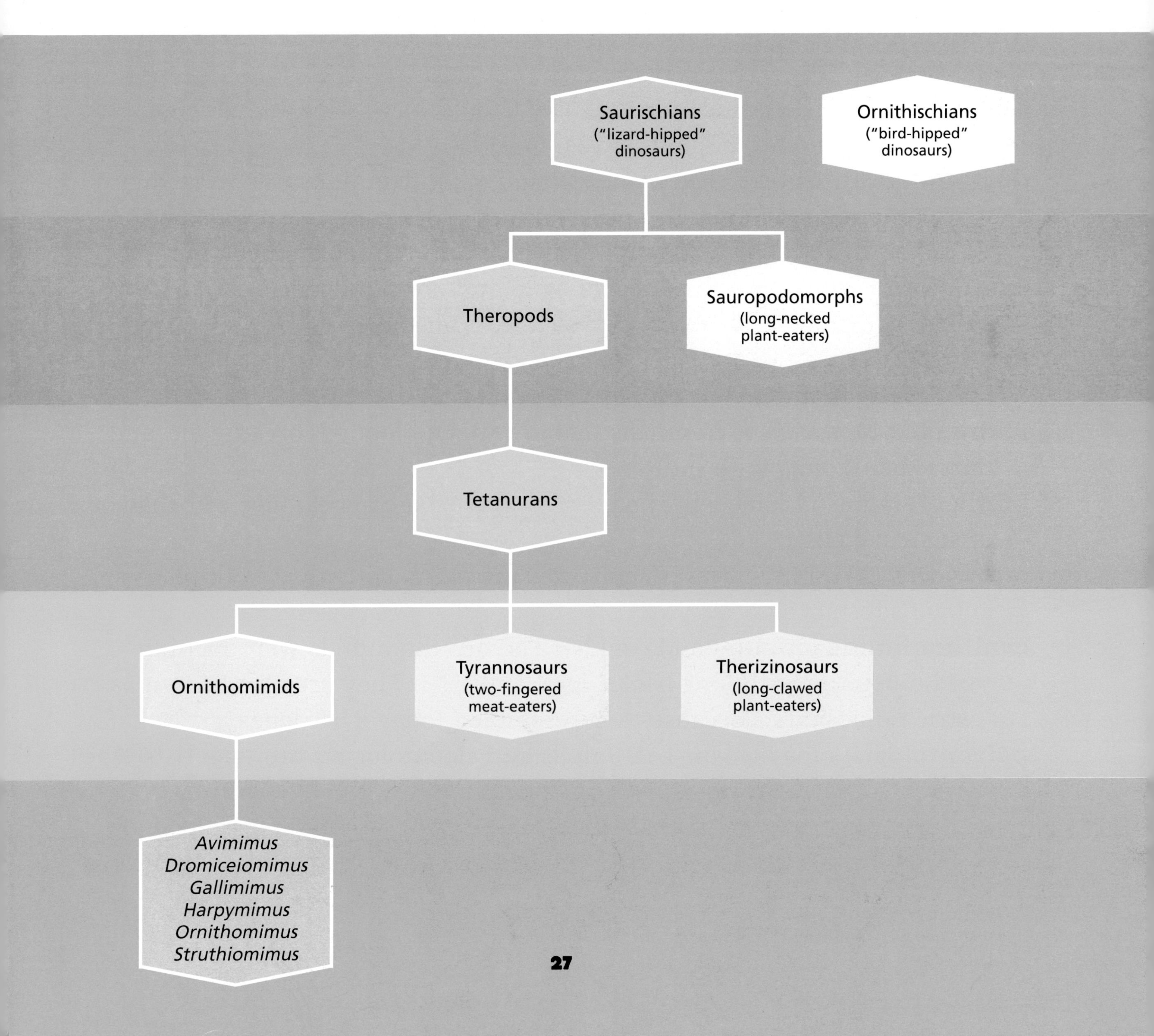

Glossary

asteroid: An asteroid is a very small planet or a fragment of a planet orbiting the sun.

Cretaceous (krih-TAY-shus) **period:** The Cretaceous period lasted from about 135 million to 65 million years ago.

duck-billed dinosaurs: The plant-eating duck-billed dinosaurs were the most common land animals on Earth during the Late Cretaceous period. They had bulky bodies, long flat beaks, and hundreds of cheek teeth.

extinction: Extinction means becoming extinct, or no longer existing. An animal is extinct when every one of its kind has died.

fossils: Fossils are the hardened remains or traces of animals or plants that lived many thousands or millions of years ago.

mammals: Mammals are animals that are warm-blooded, breathe air, and nurse their young with milk.

mimic: A mimic is someone who closely imitates the appearance or behavior of someone else.

omnivores (AHM-nih-vores)**:** Omnivores are animals that eat both plant and animal substances.

ornithomimids (or-nith-oh-MY-mids)**:** The ornithomimids were medium-sized dinosaurs with long necks, legs, and tails. They are also known as "ostrich dinosaurs," because they resembled today's ostriches.

paleontologists (pay-lee-on-TAH-luh-jists)**:** Paleontologists are scientists who study fossils to learn about dinosaurs and other forms of prehistoric life.

predators: Predators are animals that hunt and kill other animals for food.

prey: Animals that are hunted by a predator for food are the predator's prey.

Find Out More

Books

Duchesne, Lucie, and Andrew Leitch. *Jurassic Park: Gallimimus.* Universal City, CA: Amblin Entertainment, 1993.

Keiran, Monique. *Ornithomimus: Pursuing the Bird-Mimic Dinosaur.* Discoveries in Palaeontology series. Vancouver, BC: Raincoast Books, 2001.

Lessem, Don. *Ornithomimids: The Fastest Dinosaur.* Minneapolis, MN: Carolrhoda Books, 1996.

———. *Scholastic Dinosaurs A to Z.* New York: Scholastic Books, 2003.

Marshall, Chris, ed. *Dinosaurs of the World.* 11 volumes. New York: Marshall Cavendish, 1999.

Parker, Steve. *Dinosaur Pack-Hunters.* Volume 8, *The Age of the Dinosaurs.* Danbury, CT: Grolier Educational, 2000.

Online Sources*

***Dino Russ's Lair* at http://www.isgs.uiuc.edu/dinos**

Created by geologist Russ Jacobson, this Web site offers an excellent collection of links to museums and other organizations providing online information on a variety of dinosaur-related topics.

***Download-a-Dinosaur* at http://www.rain.org/~philfear/download-a-dinosaur.html**

This Schoolzone-recommended site provides free downloadable printouts of dinosaurs. Click on "A Flock of Ornithomimus" for a page that you can print, color, cut, and fold to make a group of three "bird mimics."

*Web site addresses sometimes change. The addresses here were all available when this book was sent to press. For more online sources, check with the media specialist at your local library.

***Journey through Time* at http://www.nhm.org/journey**

Presented by the Natural History Museum of Los Angeles County, California, this site offers facts and illustrations relating to dinosaurs and other prehistoric animals. Click on "Saurischian Dinosaurs" and then on "Ornithomimosaurs" for information pages on *Ornithomimus* and its cousin *Struthiomimus.*

***Jurassic Park Institute* at http://www.jpinstitute.com/index.jsp**

This entertaining Web site from Universal Studios offers lots of information for dinosaur fans. You can read about recent discoveries in "Dino News," print out dinosaur trading cards in "Dinopedia," or click on "Dinotainment" for games, puzzles, quizzes, and free dinosaur greeting cards.

***Kids' Zone* at http://www.dinosaurvalley.com/kidzone.html**

Learn about *Ornithomimus* and other dinosaurs that have been discovered in Alberta, Canada. This site created by the Royal Tyrrell Museum of Palaeontology includes lots of easy-to-read information on dinosaurs and dinosaur hunting, plus a coloring book and other activities.

***Zoom Dinosaurs* at http://www.zoomdinosaurs.com**

This colorful site from Enchanted Learning Software offers a wide variety of dinosaur-related resources, including an illustrated dictionary, information on anatomy and behavior, puzzles, quizzes, jokes, crafts, tips on writing a school report, and more.

Index

About the Author

Virginia Schomp grew up in a quiet suburban town in northeastern New Jersey where eight-ton duck-billed dinosaurs once roamed. In first grade, she discovered that she loved reading and writing, and in sixth grade she was voted "class bookworm," because she always had her nose in a book. Today she is a freelance writer who has published more than fifty books for young readers on topics including animals, careers, American history, and ancient cultures. Ms. Schomp lives in the Catskill Mountain region of New York State with her husband, Richard, and their son, Chip.

Dinosaurs lived millions of years ago. Everything we know about them—how they looked, walked, ate, fought, mated, and raised their young—comes from educated guesses by the scientists who discover and study fossils. The information in this book is based on what most scientists believe right now. Tomorrow or next week or next year, new discoveries could lead to new ideas. So keep your eyes and ears open for news flashes from the prehistoric world!

Marshall Cavendish Benchmark
99 White Plains Road
Tarrytown, New York 10591-9001
www.marshallcavendish.us

Map and Dinosaur Family Tree by Robert Romagnoli

Library of Congress Cataloging-in-Publication Data
Schomp, Virginia.
Ornithomimus : and other speedy "ostrich dinosaurs" / by Virginia Schomp.
p. cm. — (Prehistoric world)
Includes bibliographical references and index.
Summary: "Describes the physical characteristics and behavior of Ornithomimus and other speedy 'ostrich dinosaurs'"—Provided by publisher.
ISBN 0-7614-2006-1
1. Ornithomimus—Juvenile literature. 2. Dinosaurs—Juvenile literature.
I. Title. II. Series.
QE862.S3S386 2005
567.912—dc22
2004027725

Front cover: *Ornithomimus* Back cover: *Avimimus* Page 2: *Gallimimus*

Front cover illustration by Jan Sovak
Back cover illustration courtesy of Marshall Cavendish Corporation
The illustrations and photographs on the following pages are used by permission and through the courtesy of: De Agostini/Natural History Museum Picture Library, London: 2; Jan Sovak: 7, 17; Joe Tucciarone of Interstellar Illustrations: 8; Marshall Cavendish Corporation: 4–5, 11, 12–13, 15, 18–19, 20–21, 22, 23; Royal Tyrrell Museum/Alberta Community Development: 25

Printed in China

1 3 5 6 4 2